J 597.3 Wat
Waters,
Sharks

W9-AQK-612

$6.99
ocn881469614
First edition.   07/30/2015

SHARKS
HAVE SIX SENSES

JOHN F. WATERS · ILLUSTRATED BY BOB BARNER

HARPER

An Imprint of HarperCollinsPublishers

In memory of John F. Waters, 1930–2012, who greatly
admired these magnificent predators of the sea

For C.B., J.B., E.B., and M.M.
—B.B.

Special thanks to George H. Burgess, Director of the Florida
Program for Shark Research at the Florida Museum of
Natural History at the University of Florida.

The Let's-Read-and-Find-Out Science book series was originated by Dr. Franklyn M. Branley, Astronomer Emeritus and former Chairman of the American Museum–Hayden Planetarium, and was formerly co-edited by him and Dr. Roma Gans, professor Emeritus of Childhood Education, Teachers College, Columbia University. Text and illustrations for each of the books in the series are checked for accuracy by an expert in the relevant field. For more information about Let's-Read-and-Find-Out Science books, write to HarperCollins Children's Books, 195 Broadway, New York, NY 10007, or visit our website at www.readcommoncore.com.

Library of Congress Cataloging-in-Publication Data
Waters, John F., date.
  Sharks have six senses / by John F. Waters ; illustrated by Bob Barner. — First edition.
    pages cm. — (Let's-read-and-find-out science)
  Audience: Ages 4–8.
  Audience: K to grade 3.
  ISBN 978-0-06-028140-3 (hardcover) — ISBN 978-0-06-445191-8 (pbk.)
  1. Sharks—Sense organs—Juvenile literature. 2. Sharks—Juvenile literature. 3. Senses and sensation—Juvenile literature. I. Barner, Bob, illustrator. II. Title.
  QL638.9.W39 2015
  597.3 W
                                                                                              2014022687
                                                                                                      CIP
                                                                                                       AC

The artist used cut paper collage and pastels to create the illustrations for this book.

Typography by Sarah Creech

15 16 17 18 19 SCP 10 9 8 7 6 5 4 3 2 1
❖
First Edition

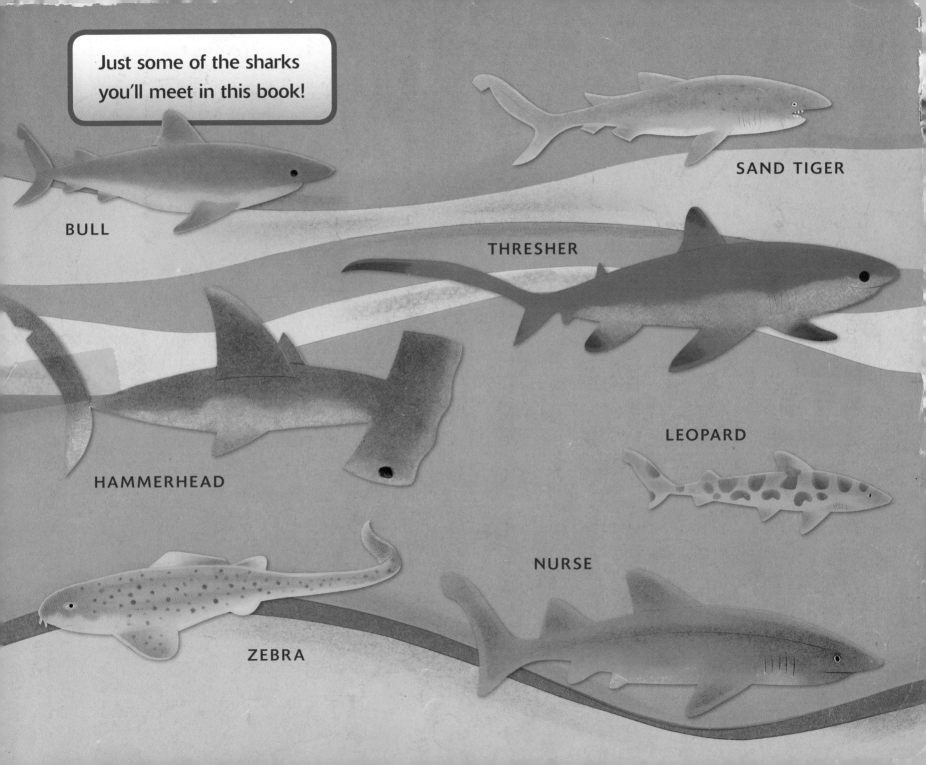

One morning a little flatfish swims along the ocean floor. Suddenly it senses danger and buries itself beneath the sand.

Along comes a hammerhead shark. The shark is looking for a meal. Because the little fish is hidden underneath the sand, the shark can't see or hear it. The shark sweeps its head back and forth, like a beachcomber with a metal detector looking for coins. It swoops down in the direction of the hidden fish. The shark bites into the sand. In a gulp or two, it eats the little fish.

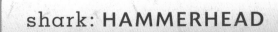

shark: HAMMERHEAD

How did the shark know that the little fish was there? It's because sharks have six senses.

The hammerhead shark is one of about 400 different kinds of sharks in the world's oceans. And no matter where in the world they live, sharks excite people.

Why? Like lions and wolves, sharks are **predators**, animals that hunt their **prey**. But sharks live in the sea and are often seen swimming near shore.

shark: THRESHER

11

In the ocean, sharks are near the top of the **food chain**. This means that there is almost nothing in the sea that eats sharks, except for bigger sharks and orca whales.

When they are looking for a meal, they are very good at what they do. If a shark is hungry, nothing can hide from it or escape it. How come? Over millions of years sharks have developed their senses to become kings of the oceans.

shark: BULL

13

Sharks have a very strong sense of smell. Some people call sharks "swimming noses," because a shark's nose is used only for smelling. Humans have to use their noses for both smelling *and* breathing. But sharks use their **gills**, which are organs that help them breathe by taking oxygen from the water.

Sharks can smell the tiniest bit of fish blood and follow it through the waves.
How tiny? Scientists did tests. They found that some sharks could smell just ten drops of blood in an area the size of a swimming pool.

sharks: SAND TIGER

Another amazing sense that sharks have is called distant touch. If a fish hides in a clump of seaweed, a shark that swims by will feel that the fish is there.

How? The shark feels its presence, because of the water current that moves against the fish and bounces off it. A shark's skin is very sensitive and can pick up very small changes in water current and temperature.

A shark's hearing is also strong. Just like a fox, a shark has very powerful hearing. But unlike foxes, sharks don't have outer ears. They have inner ears. These pick up sound vibrations. The sound vibrations go through two small pores at the top of the shark's head. Then the vibrations enter passageways that connect to the shark's inner ears.

shark: ZEBRA

Hearing is the first sense that lets sharks know where prey is when it is far away. Prey are the animals that predators hunt and eat. Sharks can hear fish before they can smell them. This is because of their inner ears and also because sound travels farther and is louder in water than it is in air. Sharks pick up the sounds of their prey looking for and munching on food. They can also hear when other sharks have found fish to eat. That's because when fish are being chased or are wounded, they swim differently and give off irregular sounds. Sharks follow all these sounds to find the fish.

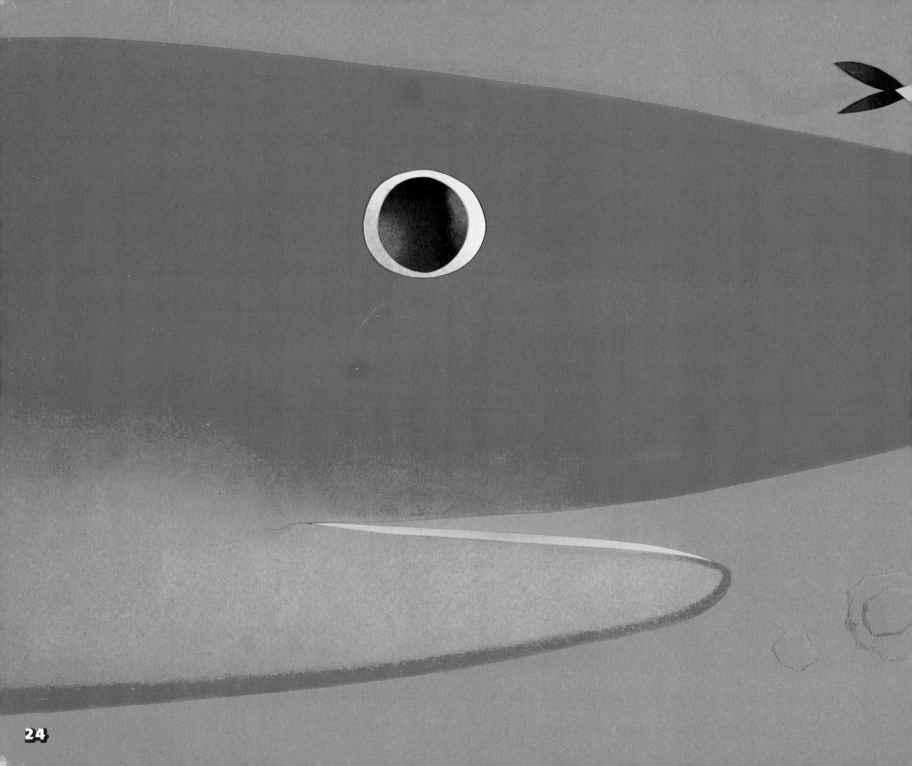

A shark's sight is good. Many sharks can see their prey up to 100 feet away.

Did you know that sharks can see in the dark? Their eyes have a special layer of tissue. So scientists believe that many kinds of sharks, like cats, can see in the dimmest light.

shark: BLUE

Once a shark has attacked an animal, either a fish or a seal, it can taste what it has caught. The shark's taste buds are in its throat and mouth, because sharks don't have tongues. These taste buds are in little knobs called **nodes**. Scientists have seen shark taste buds at work. A whitetip reef shark was seen trying to eat a Moses sole. The Moses sole is a fish that gives off bad-tasting slime. After one bite, the whitetip reef shark spit out the Moses sole. The shark swam off at great speed with its mouth wide open, trying to wash the bad taste out!

But what about that hammerhead shark that was able to find the little fish in the sand? Remember, the shark could not see, smell, or hear it. And the fish was buried in the sand, so the shark couldn't use distant touch. It used another sense.

Sharks have the same five senses as we humans. But they have an extra sixth sense! It is called **electroreception**. This allows them to sense electric fields given off by their prey.

All animals on land or in the ocean create electric fields as they move. Even a heartbeat causes an electric field. Sharks use this sense to find prey.

Good as they are at finding prey, sharks are not eating machines. They eat only when they're hungry. Sometimes days or even weeks pass between meals for large sharks.

Shark scientists believe sharks are in trouble. People kill 30–70 million sharks every year. So some kinds of sharks may not be around in a hundred years unless we act soon.

Some people may say sharks are frightening. But throughout the entire world there are only about 70 shark attacks a year. Of that, only 5 or 6 people die each year. Sharks do not want to eat people. It's common sense.

With their strong senses, big sharks could eat all the people they wanted, maybe millions of people each year. But they don't, because sharks know that people don't live in their world. Remember, most of the time, big fish eat little fish.

Sharks are truly extraordinary. Their six senses make sharks one of the most powerful creatures on land or sea!

shark: NURSE

33

FIND OUT MORE ABOUT SHARKS

There's a lot of cool information about sharks floating out there—but not all of it is true! Can you guess which ones are fact and which are fiction?

SHARKS: TRUE OR FALSE?

1) Sharks are older than dinosaurs.
TRUE! Believe it or not, scientists have found evidence to support their belief that sharks have lived on Earth for more than 400 million years. That's 200 million years before the dinosaurs were around!

2) Sharks have bony skeletons.
FALSE! A shark does not have a single bone in its body! Its skeleton is instead made of a lighter tissue called **cartilage**.

3) Sharks sleep with their eyes open.
TRUE! Like fishes, most sharks don't have eyelids, so they can't close their eyes. When sharks sleep, one side of their brain is still awake so they can continue to breathe as they rest.

4) Sharks can only be found in salt water.
FALSE! In addition to living in six of the seven oceans (including the Arctic!), several species of shark, like the bull shark, live in freshwater rivers.

5) Shark teeth are just as hard as human teeth.
TRUE! The reason sharks cut their food with their teeth and humans need to use knives to cut food is because of the different ways our teeth are shaped. It's not because human teeth are any less tough!

SHARKS AT RISK

*Sharks have been around for millions of years, but their numbers are now dwindling. The biggest threats are shark fisheries, environmental pollution, and **bycatch** (when sharks are accidentally caught and killed in fishing nets meant for tuna and other fish).*

Want to help save our sharks? Here are some things you can do to help!

- **Volunteer!** Look up shark conservation organizations and see how you can get involved.
- **Learn more about sharks!** Read books, ask your teachers, and search the internet for information. The more you know, the more you can help.

Here are some links to get you started:
World Wildlife Federation:
www.worldwildlife.org/species/shark
BBC: *www.bbc.co.uk/nature/life/shark*
Florida Museum of Natural History:
www.flmnh.ufl.edu/fish/sharks/sharks.htm

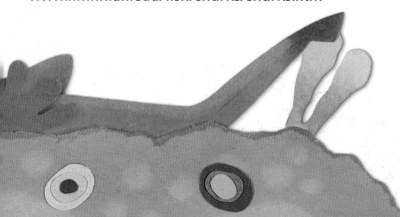

SPOT A SHARK!

Many aquariums have live web cams in their shark tanks that you can watch. Check the link below to see what it's like to "swim" with the sharks!
- Monterey Bay Aquarium:
www.montereybayaquarium.org/ animals_and_experiences/live_webcams/ open-sea-cam

Please note that all of the websites mentioned are independent from HarperCollins Publishers, and HarperCollins, the estate of John F. Waters, and Bob Barner are not responsible for any problems arising out of use of, reference to, or communication with the websites. Ask your parents before visiting any website.

This book meets the Common Core State Standards for Science and Technical Subjects. For Common Core resources for this title and others, please visit www.readcommoncore.com.

35

GLOSSARY

Bycatch: The fish and marine life that are caught unintentionally by fishing gear meant to catch other fish.

Cartilage: A tough, flexible tissue that is lighter than bone.

Electroreception: The ability to sense the natural electrical fields given off by animals.

Food chain: A system that organizes living things in order of what eats what in an ecosystem.

Gills: The organ that allows most aquatic animals to breathe by getting oxygen from water.

Nodes: Little knobs in a shark's throat and mouth containing its taste buds.

Predator: An animal that hunts and kills other animals for food.

Prey: An animal that is hunted or caught for food.

Be sure to look for all of these books in the **Let's-Read-and-Find-Out Science** series:

The Human Body:
How Many Teeth?
I'm Growing!
My Feet
My Five Senses
My Hands
Sleep Is for Everyone

Plants and Animals:
Animals in Winter
Baby Whales Drink Milk
Big Tracks, Little Tracks
Bugs Are Insects
Dinosaurs Big and Small
Ducks Don't Get Wet
Fireflies in the Night
From Caterpillar to Butterfly
From Seed to Pumpkin
From Tadpole to Frog
How Animal Babies Stay Safe
How a Seed Grows
A Nest Full of Eggs
Starfish
A Tree Is a Plant
What Lives in a Shell?
What's Alive?
What's It Like to Be a Fish?
Where Are the Night Animals?
Where Do Chicks Come From?

The World Around Us:
Air Is All Around You
The Big Dipper
Clouds
Is There Life in Outer Space?
Pop!
Snow Is Falling
Sounds All Around
What Makes a Shadow?

The Human Body:
A Drop of Blood
Germs Make Me Sick!
Hear Your Heart
The Skeleton Inside You
What Happens to a Hamburger?
Why I Sneeze, Shiver, Hiccup, and Yawn
Your Skin and Mine

Plants and Animals:
Almost Gone
Ant Cities
Be a Friend to Trees
Chirping Crickets
Corn Is Maize
Dolphin Talk
Honey in a Hive
How Do Apples Grow?
How Do Birds Find Their Way?
Life in a Coral Reef
Look Out for Turtles!
Milk from Cow to Carton
An Octopus Is Amazing
Penguin Chick
Sharks Have Six Senses
Snakes Are Hunters
Spinning Spiders
Sponges Are Skeletons
What Color Is Camouflage?
Who Eats What?
Who Lives in an Alligator Hole?
Why Do Leaves Change Color?
Why Frogs Are Wet
Wiggling Worms at Work
Zipping, Zapping, Zooming Bats

Dinosaurs:
Did Dinosaurs Have Feathers?
Digging Up Dinosaurs
Dinosaur Bones
Dinosaur Tracks
Dinosaurs Are Different
Fossils Tell of Long Ago
My Visit to the Dinosaurs
What Happened to the Dinosaurs?
Where Did Dinosaurs Come From?

Space:
Floating in Space
The International Space Station
Mission to Mars
The Moon Seems to Change
The Planets in Our Solar System
The Sky Is Full of Stars
The Sun
What Makes Day and Night
What the Moon Is Like

Weather and the Seasons:
Down Comes the Rain
Feel the Wind
Flash, Crash, Rumble, and Roll
Hurricane Watch
Sunshine Makes the Seasons
Tornado Alert
What Will the Weather Be?

Our Earth:
Archaeologists Dig for Clues
Earthquakes
Follow the Water from Brook to Ocean
How Mountains Are Made
In the Rainforest
Let's Go Rock Collecting
Oil Spill!
Volcanoes
What Happens to Our Trash?
What's So Bad About Gasoline?
Where Do Polar Bears Live?
Why Are the Ice Caps Melting?
You're Aboard Spaceship Earth

The World Around Us:
Day Light, Night Light
Energy Makes Things Happen
Forces Make Things Move
Gravity Is a Mystery
How People Learned to Fly
Light Is All Around Us
Switch On, Switch Off
What Is the World Made Of?
What Makes a Magnet?
Where Does the Garbage Go?